ELMER
David McKee

for Brett

HarperCollins*Publishers*

There was once a herd of elephants. Elephants young,
elephants old, elephants tall and short, fat and thin.
All were different but all were happy and almost all
were the same color.

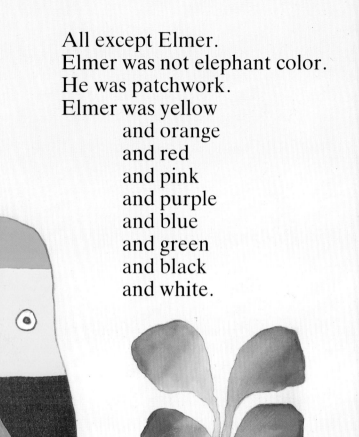

All except Elmer.
Elmer was not elephant color.
He was patchwork.
Elmer was yellow
         and orange
         and red
         and pink
         and purple
         and blue
         and green
         and black
         and white.

It was Elmer who kept the other elephants happy. Their games and jokes were always his idea. If an elephant was laughing, the cause was usually Elmer.

But Elmer himself wasn't happy. "Whoever heard of a patchwork elephant?" he thought. "No wonder they laugh at me!" One morning, just as the others were waking up. Elmer slipped away.

As he walked through the jungle, Elmer met other animals.

"Good morning, Elmer," they said.

After a long walk Elmer found what he was looking for – a large bush covered with elephant-colored berries. Elmer caught hold of the bush and shook it until the berries fell on the ground.

Then Elmer lay down and rolled over on the
berries, this way and that. He picked up
bunches of berries and rubbed himself all
over until he was covered with berry juice.
When he had finished, there wasn't a sign
of any yellow, or orange, or red, or pink,
or purple, or blue, or green, or black, or
white. Elmer looked like any other elephant.

On his way back through the jungle, Elmer passed
the other animals.

"Good morning, elephant," they said.

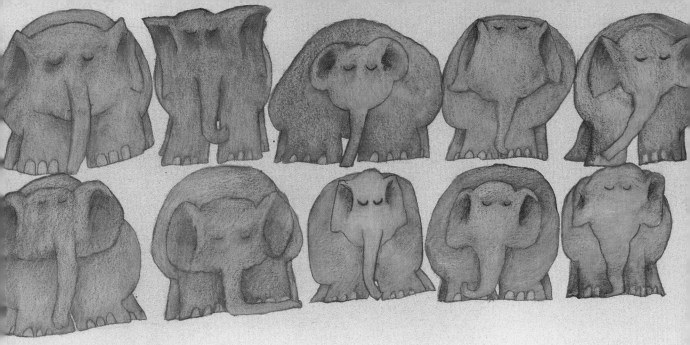

When Elmer rejoined the herd, none of
the other elephants noticed him.

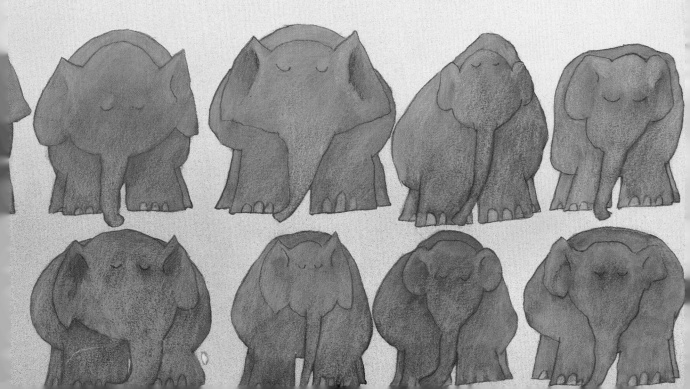

As he stood there, Elmer felt that something was wrong. But what?

He looked around: same old jungle, same old
blue sky, same old rain cloud, same old elephants.

The other elephants were standing absolutely
still, silent and serious. Elmer had never seen
them so serious before. It made him want to laugh.
Finally he could bear it no longer. He lifted his
trunk and, at the top of his voice, shouted –

The other elephants jumped in surprise. Elmer
was helpless with laughter. Then the others
began to laugh.

"Too bad Elmer isn't here to share the fun,"
they said, laughing harder and harder.

And then the rain cloud burst. When the rain
fell on Elmer, his patchwork started to show
again. "Oh, Elmer," gasped an old elephant as
Elmer was washed back to normal. "You've played
some good jokes, but this has been the biggest
laugh of all. What would we do without you?"

"We must celebrate this day every year," said
another. "The day of Elmer's best joke."
"All of us elephants will decorate ourselves
in his honor," said a third. "And Elmer will
decorate himself elephant color."

And one day each year the elephants color themselves yellow, or orange, or red, or pink, or purple, or blue, or green, or black, or white and have a parade. If you happen to see an elephant in the Elmer's Day parade who is ordinary elephant color, you will know it must be Elmer.

Library of Congress Cataloging-in-Publication Data
McKee, David.
Originally published: New York: McGraw-Hill, 1968.
Summary: All the elephants of the jungle were gray except Elmer,
who was a patchwork of brilliant colors until the day he got tired of
being different and making the other elephants laugh.
[1. Elephants—Fiction.] I. Title. PZ7.M19448El 1989
[E] 89-2285

U.S. Edition 1 2 3 4 5 6 7 8 9 10

Manufactured in China by South China Printing Company Ltd.
First paper-over-board edition, 2004